Merry Christmas To All

ISBN 0-590-48476-1

Copyright © 1994 by Scholastic Inc.

All rights reserved. Published by Scholastic Inc.

CARTWHEEL BOOKS is a registered trademark of Scholastic Inc.

12 11 10 9 8 7 6 5 4 3 2 1   4 5 6 7 8 9/9

Printed in Singapore

First Scholastic printing, October 1994

Merry Christmas To All

A Collection of Favorite Christmas Stories, Poems,
and Songs for the Holiday Season

SCHOLASTIC INC. Cartwheel B·O·O·K·S®

New York Toronto London Auckland Sydney

Contents

III. Happy Ho-Ho-Ho Holidays!

IV. Christmas Songs and Carols

I

Classic Tales of Christmas

THE NUTCRACKER BALLET

adapted by Carol Thompson
Illustrated by Darcy May

It was Christmas Eve. Marie and Fritz could hardly wait for the Christmas party to begin!

Behind the closed doors of the living room, their parents were decorating for the party. Marie peeked through the keyhole, trying to catch a glimpse of the Christmas tree.

Soon the guests arrived, and the big doors were opened wide. There in the middle of the room stood the most beautiful tree Marie and Fritz had ever seen!

It sparkled with the light of a hundred candles. Toys, cookies, and candy canes hung from the branches. Underneath the tree were colorful gifts of all shapes and sizes, and a golden star was shining brightly at the top.

Godfather Drosselmeyer walked into the room, and the guests began to whisper excitedly. Drosselmeyer was a famous toymaker. His toys seemed almost magical!

Some of the children were afraid of Drosselmeyer, with his wild white hair and his black eye patch. But Marie loved him dearly.

Drosselmeyer brought in two big boxes. All the guests gathered around to see what wonderful toys he had made. Slowly, he opened the green box. A toy ballerina leapt out and started to dance!

Then Drosselmeyer untied the red ribbon, and a big toy soldier kicked open the box and began marching. Everyone clapped and cheered.

Drosselmeyer gave his goddaughter a special present. It was a wooden nutcracker shaped like a little soldier.

Naughty Fritz snatched the nutcracker away . . . and stuffed a big walnut into its mouth.

CRACK! CRACK! CRACK!

Three teeth fell out!

"Stop it, Fritz!" Marie cried.

"It's an ugly thing," said Fritz, "and it doesn't even work!"

Marie took the nutcracker away from Fritz and hugged it tightly. "Never mind," she whispered to the nutcracker. "I'll always take care of you."

Drosselmeyer helped Marie tie a handkerchief around the nutcracker's jaw. "Don't worry," he said. "Your nutcracker will be all right after a good night's rest."

Soon the party was over and the children went off to bed.

But Marie couldn't sleep. She crept downstairs to see her nutcracker one more time. On the floor beside his little bed, she fell fast asleep. Marie didn't see Godfather Drosselmeyer come into the room and fix the nutcracker's jaw.

The clock chimed midnight. Marie woke with a start, not knowing where she was. She looked around the dark room and realized that everything around her was growing bigger!

The Christmas tree towered above her. The toys under the tree were nearly her size, and so was the nutcracker!

Suddenly Marie heard the sound of footsteps. She turned and saw an army of huge mice charging toward the toys!

The nutcracker drew his sword and led the toy soldiers into battle. The other toys followed, and soon teddy bears, dolls, and puppets all had joined in the fight against the mice.

Something whizzed past Marie's head. The dolls were firing gumdrops from the toy cannon!

The toys fought hard, but there were too many mice. Then the King of the Mice knocked the nutcracker down. With an evil laugh, he raised his sword above the nutcracker's head.

Oh no! thought Marie. *I must do something.* She took off her slipper

and threw it at the Mouse King. The shoe hit his head and knocked him off balance.

The nutcracker quickly jumped up and attacked the king. In the wink of an eye, the Mouse King was dead, and the battle was over!

The nutcracker took the Mouse King's crown so he could give it to Marie. But Marie was lying on the bed. She had fainted from all the excitement!

The nutcracker climbed onto the bed and stood at the head, as if he were captain of a sailing ship. He pointed his sword at the window, and it swung open. Then the bed sailed away, across the starry sky.

Soon the bed came to rest in a snowy woods. Marie awoke and saw that her nutcracker had changed into a handsome prince.

He smiled at her and said, "My dear Marie, thank you for helping me win the battle. Now let me take you to my kingdom, the Land of Sweets."

The nutcracker took Marie's hand and led her through the woods to his palace. The beautiful Sugar Plum Fairy was waiting at the gate to meet them.

The Sugar Plum Fairy showed Marie and the Nutcracker Prince into a sparkling crystal hall where they sat upon a huge golden throne.

"Let the festivities begin!" said the Sugar Plum Fairy. All the happy people of the Land of Sweets came to dance in honor of the Prince's return.

First a beautifully dressed couple did the dance of hot chocolate. Then came the dance of coffee, with a dancer who twirled and leapt high into the air.

A pair in silken costumes from China jumped out of an enormous teapot to perform the dance of tea.

Mother Ginger swept into the hall wearing a large hoopskirt which hid a surprise — a band of mischievous children who did a merry dance!

At last all of the flowers of the land came to perform a lovely waltz. Their swirling colors and sweet perfume made Marie dizzy with happiness.

"What a beautiful place this is," sighed Marie. "Promise you'll bring me back here someday."

"You can always visit in your dreams," said the Nutcracker Prince with a smile.

All too soon, it was time for Marie to go home. She and the prince stepped into his magic sleigh and waved farewell.

"Good-bye! Good luck!" called the people of the Land of Sweets as the sleigh carried Marie and the prince high above the clouds.

The next morning, Marie woke up and found the nutcracker in her arms.

"You're as good as new!" she exclaimed. "Just as Godfather Drosselmeyer said you would be!"

Marie smiled and hugged her precious nutcracker, thinking of her wonderful night in the Land of Sweets. Had her adventure been only a dream . . . or a bit of Christmas magic?

THE LITTLE MATCH GIRL

adapted by Amanda Stephens
Illustrated by Lucinda McQueen

"Matches for sale. Beautiful bundles of matches for sale . . ."

The young girl looked hopeful as she held out a bundle of matches tied with a red ribbon. Perhaps the people hurrying by would take pity on her and buy some of her wares. But the passersby barely paid her any mind. After all, it was Christmas Eve, and they had parties to go to, presents to wrap, and trees to trim. They had no time to stop and buy matches from a poor, motherless Little Match Girl.

The Little Match Girl pulled her tattered cape around her shoulders and shivered. The bitter wind blew through the holes in her threadbare dress; the snow seeped through the thin soles of her shoes. The Little Match Girl sighed. If only she could sell a few of her matches. Then she could buy some food for her father and herself. But sadly, she had not sold one bundle of matches all day. She could not go home without any money — not on Christmas Eve! So ever so slowly, she walked on, crying out: "Matches for sale. Beautiful bundles of matches . . ."

Clickety clack . . . Clickety clack . . . The Little Match Girl looked up in surprise. A horsedrawn carriage was coming quickly down the road.

"Out of my way, street urchin!" the driver yelled at the Little Match Girl.

The child leaped out of the way of the oncoming carriage. But her shoes were far too big for her feet, and she tripped and fell — spilling her matches all over the freshly fallen snow. As she crawled around picking them up, two cruel boys grabbed her shoes and ran off laughing into the night. The poor little girl had no choice but to walk barefoot through the ice and snow.

The snow was falling very hard now, and the Little Match Girl could hardly see. She found herself some shelter in a corner formed by two large buildings. She huddled against the bricks, trying to keep warm. But the bricks were cold, and the ground was wet. The Little Match Girl looked down at her basket of wooden matches.

Perhaps I should light just one match, she thought. *At least I could warm my hands by its flame.* With cold and icy fingers, she took a match from its bundle and struck it.

The little flame flickered at first, and then burst into a glorious pink light. The Little Match Girl looked with surprise at the sight that appeared before her eyes. There was a delicious Christmas dinner, laid out on a brilliant white lace tablecloth. The main course was a fat, crispy roast duckling surrounded by sweet candied yams and tart red cranberry sauce. The Little Match Girl had never seen such a splendid meal! But just as she reached out to take just a bit of the tasty duckling, the candle sputtered and went out, taking the sumptuous banquet with it.

Deep inside, the Little Match Girl knew her father would be angry if she came home without matches or money, but she could not think about that now. Instead, she took another match from the bundle and struck it. Within an instant, the tiny flame burst into a bright-green haze. In the center of the haze was the most beautiful Christmas tree The Little Match Girl had ever seen. The large fir was trimmed with silver, sparkly tinsel. Red and green ornaments hung from every branch, and a hundred candles glowed into the night. Quickly, the Little Match Girl moved toward the candles. But just as quickly, the match sputtered and died out, leaving the Little Match Girl cold and alone once more.

Once again, the child lit a match. And this time she saw the greatest sight of all — her beloved grandmother who had left her and gone to heaven two Christmases before. Frantically, the shivering child reached out to the old woman. "Oh, Grandmother," she called out. "You look so warm and lovely. And I have missed you so. Please, do not leave me."

The child reached into her basket once more. *Perhaps if I light all of the matches*, she thought, *my grandmother will keep me warm for the night.* And with that, she lit all of her matches, one by one.

When she got to the last match, she cried out. "Take me with you, Grandmother. Take me where it is warm and peaceful. But hurry — this last match will soon die out and I shall never see you again."

The old woman swept her granddaughter up in her arms. In a light as bright as ten thousand matches, they soared together up to heaven. The angels greeted them with open arms, wrapping the child's shivering body in warm, woolen fleece. Never again would the poor child be hungry or cold. Now she was home — safe with her grandmother and the angels.

THE ELVES AND THE SHOEMAKER

adapted by Freya Littledale
Illustrated by Brinton Turkle

There was once a good shoemaker who became very poor.

At last he had only one piece of leather to make one pair of shoes.

"Well," said the shoemaker to his wife, "I will cut the leather tonight and make the shoes in the morning."

The next morning he went to his table, and he couldn't believe what he saw.

The leather was polished. The sewing was done. And there was a fine pair of shoes! Not one stitch was out of place.

"Do you see what I see?" asked the shoemaker.

"Indeed I do," said his wife. "I see a fine pair of shoes."

"But who could have made them?" the shoemaker said.

"It's just like magic!" said his wife.

At that very moment a man came in with a top hat and cane. "Those shoes look right for me," said the man.

And so they were. They were right from heel to toe.

"How much do they cost?"

"One gold coin," said the shoemaker.

"I'll give you two," said the man.

And he went on his way with a smile on his face and the new shoes on his feet.

"Well, well," said the shoemaker, "now I can buy leather for two pairs of shoes." And he cut the leather that night so he could make the shoes in the morning.

The next morning the shoemaker woke up, and he found two pairs of ladies' shoes. They were shining in the sunlight.

"Who is making these shoes?" said the shoemaker. "They are the best shoes in the world."

At that very moment two ladies came in. They looked exactly alike. "My, what pretty shoes!" said the ladies. "They will surely fit us."

And the ladies were right.

They gave the shoemaker four gold coins and away they went . . . *clickety-clack, clickety-clack* in their pretty shoes.

And so it went. Every night the shoemaker cut the leather. Every morning the shoes were made. And every day more people came to buy his beautiful shoes. Just before Christmas the shoemaker said, "Whoever is making these shoes is making us very happy."

"And rich," said his wife.

"Let us stay up and see who it is," the shoemaker said.

"Good," said his wife.

So they hid behind some coats, and they waited and waited and waited.

When the clock struck twelve, in came the two little elves.
"Elves," cried the shoemaker.
"Shh!" said his wife.
At once the elves hopped up on the table and set to work.

Tap-tap went their hammers.
Snip-snap went their scissors.
Stitch-stitch went their needles.

Their tiny fingers moved so fast the shoemaker and his wife could hardly believe their eyes.

The elves sewed and they hammered and they didn't stop until all the shoes were finished. There were little shoes and big ones. There were white ones and black ones and brown ones.

The elves lined them all in a row. Then they jumped down from the table. They ran across the room and out the door.

The next morning the wife said, "The elves have made us very happy. I want to make them happy, too. They need new clothes to keep warm.

"So I'll make them pants and shirts and coats. And I'll knit them socks and hats. You can make them each a pair of shoes."

"Yes, yes!" said the shoemaker. And they went right to work.

On Christmas Eve the shoemaker left no leather on the table. He left all the pretty gifts instead.

Then he and his wife hid behind the coats to see what the elves would do.

When the clock struck twelve, in came the elves, ready to set to work.

But when they looked at the table and saw the fine clothes, they laughed and clapped their hands.

"How happy they are!" said the shoemaker's wife.

"Shhh," said her husband. The elves put on the clothes, looked in the mirror, and began to sing:

> *What fine and handsome elves are we,*
> *No longer cobblers will we be.*
> *From now on we'll dance and play,*
> *Into the woods and far away.*

They hopped over the table and jumped over the chairs.

They skipped all around the room, danced out the door, and were never seen again.

But from that night on everything always went well for the good shoemaker and his wife.

BABES IN TOYLAND

adapted by Gina Shaw
Illustrated by John Speirs

"Come, children! Gather 'round! Help me prepare the village square!" called Mother Goose. Her children raced from all directions.

Jack and Jill came down from the hill. Little Miss Muffett jumped up from her tuffet. Little Bo Peep stopped counting her sheep. Their other brothers and sisters came running, too.

It was the day before Christmas Eve. The children were very excited. They all wanted to help decorate Mother Goose Village for their favorite holiday.

Some children hung garlands of holly and berries on the tall Christmas tree.

Others hammered green, red, and gold wreaths on doors.

And some placed small wooden toys on the branches of the tree. What better way for Mother Goose Village, the largest town in Toyland, to celebrate Christmas than with tiny toys!

29

Contrary Mary, Mother Goose's oldest daughter, placed a bright star at the top of the tree. This was an extra-special time for her. On Christmas Day, she would marry her true love, Tom Piper. Mary's smile matched the brightness of the star.

But just as she was on her way down from the ladder, a dark cloud seemed to cover the village square. Everyone gasped. . . .

It was Barnaby, the richest, greediest, and most powerful man in Toyland. He was very unhappy. He did not want Mary to marry Tom. He wanted to marry her himself!

Barnaby had a plan, and he was about to put it into action.

"Clear the square!" bellowed Barnaby. "Christmas will *not* be celebrated this year! Take down these decorations."

Barnaby turned to Mother Goose and said, "As of today, I am charging you double your rent."

Mother Goose could not believe her ears. Then Barnaby said, "But maybe we can make a deal. Call off the wedding and you can live here rent free!"

"Tom and Mary love each other," said Mother Goose. "We can't stop their wedding."

Barnaby turned away muttering, "We'll see about that!"

Barnaby's sidekick, Roderigo, found Barnaby as he was walking home. "I took care of everything," said Roderigo. "We'll get rid of Tom tonight."

Mary heard Roderigo and Barnaby talking, and she stopped them.

"What are you planning to do to Tom?" she demanded.

"My only plans are the plans for our wedding," Barnaby said slyly.

Mary wanted to get far away from these two men. She wanted to find Tom. She ran and ran without looking where she was going. The news that Mary had run away spread quickly. It even reached Tom.

Mary did not know that Barnaby and Roderigo came after her. They followed her into the deepest, darkest, and most dangerous place in all of Toyland — the Forest of No Return!

Soon the forest worked its spell on all of them, and they fell fast asleep. As they slept, gigantic spiders came out of hiding. The spiders spun silken webs tightly around each of them.

As the spiders scurried away, Tom entered the forest looking for Mary. He gasped when he saw her. Tom knelt beside Mary and gently brushed a moth from her shoulder.

Suddenly the moth fluttered its wings and changed into a beautiful butterfly. It untangled the spiderweb and lifted both Tom and Mary onto its back. Then it carried them safely out of the Forest of No Return to the doorstep of the Toymaker.

Inside the Toymaker's shop, the Toymaker and his assistant, Grumio, were busy indeed. They had to make all the Christmas toys for the boys and girls of Toyland. These two loved to tinker. Right now they were busy working on a machine that could bring toys to life!

Grumio flipped the power switch on. The great machine sputtered. A large doll came down the assembly line. Smoke was pouring out of it.

The Toymaker scratched his head. "If at first you don't succeed, Grumio, try, try again!"

Just then Mary and Tom raced through the workshop.

Grumio was joyous. "Look! Our dolls *are* coming to life!" he said.

Mary pleaded with the Toymaker. "Won't you help us? Old Barnaby is spreading unhappiness everywhere. He's trying to stop the Village Christmas celebration and our wedding!"

The wise old Toymaker said, "Don't worry! Nothing bad can happen to you here. Now pretend you are my dolls and line up with the other toys."

Tom and Mary did what the Toymaker told them to do.

At that moment, Barnaby and Roderigo burst into the Toymaker's workshop. "I know Tom and Mary are here," Barnaby shouted. "Where are they?" Then the toy machine caught his eye.

"What have we here?" asked Barnaby, walking toward the Toymaker's machine.

The Toymaker answered, "This machine makes toys!"

"Then I will make lots of toys for myself," Barnaby said with a greedy smile. He began flicking switches and turning knobs.

Suddenly toys came off in all directions — and they were coming to life! The Toymaker's machine was working after all!

"Now is your chance!" whispered the Toymaker to Tom and Mary. "Lead the toys and scare Barnaby and Roderigo away."

And that is just what they did! Barnaby couldn't believe that the toys were alive. When he saw them marching toward him, he screamed and ran. Barnaby and Roderigo ran until they reached the edge of Toyland. As they crossed the border, Tom, Mary, and all the toys began to cheer, for everyone knows that once you pass the borders of Toyland, you can never return again.

Tom and Mary went back to the workshop, and all of the toys followed. One by one, they became real toys again.

Tom and Mary hugged the Toymaker and thanked him. He gave them lots of toys to take back for the children in Mother Goose Village.

Then he said, "Have a very Merry Christmas! Always keep love in your heart."

Finally it was Christmas Day. Tom and Mary's wedding was beautiful.

And all the children had a wonderful time celebrating Christmas in Mother Goose Village!

THE STORY OF THE NATIVITY

adapted from the King James Bible, St. Luke and St. Matthew
Illustrated by Jacqueline Rogers

AND it came to pass in those days, that there went out a decree from Caesar Augustus that all the world should be taxed.

And all went to be taxed, every one into his own city.

And Joseph also went to be taxed with Mary, his espoused wife, being great with child.

And so it was that, while they were there, the days were accomplished that she should be delivered.

And she brought forth her firstborn son, and wrapped him in swaddling clothes, and laid him in a manger; because there was no room for them in the inn.

And there were in the same country shepherds abiding in the field, keeping watch over their flock by night.

And lo, the angel of the Lord came upon them, and the glory of the Lord shone round about them; and they were sore afraid.

And the angel said unto them, Fear not: for, behold, I bring you good tidings of great joy, which shall be to all people.

For unto you is born this day in the city of David a Saviour, which is Christ the Lord.

And this *shall be* a sign unto you; Ye shall find the babe wrapped in swaddling clothes, lying in a manger.

And suddenly there was with the angel a multitude of the heavenly host praising God, and saying,

Glory to God in the highest, and on earth peace, good will toward men.

And it came to pass, as the angels were gone away from them into heaven, the shepherds said one to another, Let us now go even unto Bethlehem, and see this thing which is come to pass, which the Lord hath made known unto us.

And they came with haste, and found Mary and Joseph, and the babe lying in a manger.

And when they had seen *it*, they made known abroad the saying which was told them concerning this child.

And the shepherds returned,
glorifying and praising God for all
the things that they had heard and seen,
as it was told unto them.

And there came wise men from the east
to Jerusalem,

Saying, Where is he that is born King
of the Jews? For we have seen his star
in the east, and are come to worship him.

And lo, the star, which they saw in
the east, went before them, till it came
and stood over where the young child was.

When they saw the star, they rejoiced
with exceeding great joy.

And when they were come into the
house, they saw the young child with Mary
his mother, and fell down, and worshipped
him: and when they had opened their
treasures, they presented unto him gifts:
gold, and frankincense, and myrrh.

THE LITTLE CROOKED CHRISTMAS TREE

by Michael Cutting
Illustrated by Ron Broda

Out beyond the town, where the farms begin, is an unusual field. In the early spring, when all the other fields are bare and brown, this field is green and bright because it is filled with little Christmas trees. This is the story of one special tree.

From where the little tree was growing, among the rows and rows of trees, he could at last see the big, bold letters of the sign that had puzzled him for so long. There it stood, at the end of the field — "Brown's Christmas Tree Farm."

He was sure that he was a tree, but he didn't know what a Christmas tree was, or even what Christmas was. He did know that he was supposed to grow straight and tall and healthy for some special reason.

Every few days a man would walk past and look at him. The man would pull out the weeds around his trunk and spray him all over, getting rid of the itchy bugs and the pesky caterpillars that clogged up his needles and nibbled at his bark.

By the time he was seven years old, the little tree was big enough for birds and other creatures to perch on his branches. He looked forward to the arrival of new visitors in the hope that they would be able to answer his questions about Christmas.

His first visitor was a goose, who stopped to nibble the fresh young grass by his trunk. "Please, Miss Goose," asked the tree, "what is Christmas? And what is a Christmas tree?"

"You're asking the wrong bird," said the goose. "My friends and I always go south at that time of the year."

Soon a squirrel came by, leaping from tree to tree. "Please, Mr. Squirrel, what is a Christmas tree? And what is Christmas?"

"You're asking the wrong squirrel," he said. "We always sleep through that time of year."

Then one stormy day a white dove came to rest on his topmost branch. It landed with a thump, fell off one branch through the next and the next, until the tree pulled his softest branches together to make a thick, green bed that caught and cradled the little white dove.

"Oh, thank you, little tree," said the white dove. "I'm just too, too tired to fly any further. Strong winds blew me away from my home. The beautiful nest I worked so hard on was blown right off the tree, and it's time for me to lay my eggs. Oh, little tree, can you pull your softest branches together and hold them like that as a nest for my eggs?"

For weeks and weeks the little tree struggled to keep his branches close and still as the eggs hatched and three baby doves peeped and cooed. While the busy mother dove was out hunting for seeds, the little tree made an even greater effort and pulled his branches right over them to shelter them from the sun and rain and hide them from hawks and other dangerous creatures.

The little tree worked so hard helping the white dove raise her children, always pulling his branches over to one side, that he forgot all about growing straight and tall as a Christmas tree should. Gradually he developed a big hump in his trunk.

The farmer walked past and looked disappointed, and he shook his head sadly. He stopped pulling out the weeds around the little tree's trunk. He hardly bothered to spray him for itchy bugs or nibbling caterpillars any more. The little tree felt quite neglected, but he would not give up taking care of the white dove and her children.

The day arrived when the little doves were big enough to learn to fly. They stretched their wings and flapped all the way to the next tree and back. Gradually they began to fly further, but they always came back to the little tree at dusk.

One day the mother dove said to the tree, "Oh, little tree, by saving my life and taking care of my children you've grown a big hump in your trunk. The farmer hardly bothers to pull out the weeds around you or spray your branches anymore, and it's all my fault.

"Now it's time for us to fly back to the big tree where I once lived. The people in the house nearby put out seeds everyday in the winter for me, as they did for my mother and grandmother before me. It's so hard to find food when the ground is covered in snow, and besides, I'm sure they miss us. But I promise we'll all be back to visit with you in the spring. Tell me, is there anything I can do for you before we go?"

"Please, Mrs. Dove," cried the little tree, "before you go, can you tell me what a Christmas tree is, and what Christmas is? I know that I'll never be a proper Christmas tree now, but I would still like to know what I might have been, and what all the trees I grew up with are going to be."

"Little tree," said the dove, "Christmas is a time when people celebrate the birth of Jesus Christ, who was born to bring peace to the world. Just before Christmas, families bring their children to find a nice, straight Christmas tree. They cut it down and take it home, where it is decorated with colored lights and shiny ornaments, and they place gifts around it. Grandparents and aunts and uncles and friends all come to admire the tree. Then, when the holiday is over, the lights and ornaments are put away and the poor tree is thrown out, alone, in the snow. By saving me and my children you have grown crooked, but now you are safe."

With this, the white dove and her children flew off.

The snow came, the winds howled, the pond froze. The birds flew south, the squirrels slept, nothing and no one moved on Brown's Christmas Tree Farm.

Then one day, with the snow softly falling, the field was filled with people. Mothers, fathers, children, all laughing and talking, all looking for the perfect tree to take home. Some even looked at the little tree, but when they brushed the snow from his branches and saw the hump on his trunk, they shook their heads and moved on.

But along with the laughter, the thud of axes and the sound of splitting wood filled the air. The little tree stood helpless as one by one all the other trees fell and were dragged away to the waiting cars.

That was the loneliest time of the tree's life. All that long, cold winter he stood alone with nothing to shelter him from the icy winds. When the spring came, no birds stopped by, for one lonely, crooked tree in an empty field was no place to rest on their long journey. Farmer Brown came out with some men, who planted hundreds of baby Christmas trees in rows up and down the field. No one took any notice of the little tree, except to hang their coats on his branches.

One warm and sunny morning, there was a gentle cooing and a flapping of wings. The white dove had kept her promise and had brought her children back to visit.

"Oh, I missed you so much," sobbed the little tree. "I thought that winter had taken you from me. Oh, Mrs. Dove, I'm so alone. They cut down all the friends I grew up with and took them away. No one wanted me because of the hump on my trunk. Nobody was left to shelter me from the icy winds. Farmer Brown planted rows of baby trees, but they're far too young for me to talk to. You told me that a Christmas tree only has colored lights and shiny ornaments for a short time, but I'd rather bring happiness and laughter to children for those special few days than be lonely and cold all winter by myself. Isn't that what I was made for, to be a symbol of joy and love?"

The white dove and her children comforted the little tree. They stayed with him all day, and flew off with a promise to return soon.

Summer came, and one day Farmer Brown arrived with some men, some shovels, and a strange machine. They dug and dug all around the little tree's roots. They wrapped them in damp sacking, then used the machine to lift him carefully out of the ground and onto a truck.

It was a long journey lying on his side, with the sun drying his roots and making him thirsty. Eventually the truck arrived at a big house, where a deep hole was waiting in the garden, just the shape and size of the little tree's roots. They lifted him carefully from the truck, undid the sacking, placed him in the hole, and filled in the earth around him. Then they soaked the ground with cool, fresh water. The little tree sighed and settled his roots gratefully.

The next day, he looked around at his new home. All kinds of strange flowers grew nearby. The grass was even and green, not tufted with the brown patches that he was used to. But, strangest of all, he was surrounded by the most unusual trees. The little Christmas tree had never seen anything like them. He was positively dwarfed by them! Some grew in clumps, others towered alone to the sky, and some even had flowers on their branches. There wasn't another Christmas tree in sight.

Nevertheless, it was nice to be with trees again, so he plucked up his courage and spoke to one. "Excuse me, sir. I'm a Christmas tree. Who are you?"

"Harrumph," replied the haughty birch. "You're not a real tree. You're just a scrubby little spruce with a crooked trunk and prickly needles. A real tree has silver bark and soft green leaves. You don't belong in this garden at all." With that, he turned his leaves to the sun and ignored the little tree.

Timidly, the little tree turned his branches up and spoke to the giant behind him. "Excuse me, sir. I just arrived last night. I'm a Christmas tree. Who are you?"

"By my acorns," thundered the proud oak, "real trees grow straight and tall. You're not a real tree. You're just a crooked little nothing."

And so it was with all the others. They wouldn't speak to him because he wasn't tall enough, or straight enough, or wearing the right color bark. The little Christmas tree was just as lonely as he had been in the empty field. Even the birds ignored him, preferring to perch in the branches of the taller trees.

As summer turned to autumn and nights became cold, all the trees started to change. Their greens turned to golds and browns. Leaves hung limply from branches and then fell to the ground. The giant oak shivered naked in the winter winds. The haughty birch, whose bark was not quite as fine as when there were no leaves to hide it, shook in the sleet and rain. The only one who stood green and fresh in the garden was the little Christmas tree.

Even as autumn turned to winter, and the rain turned to snow, the little tree stood proudly green and fresh, with a lacy coat of fluffy white snow on his branches.

One cold day the people of the house came out to the little tree with big boxes full of beautiful things. They hung strings and strings of colored lights from his branches, and they decorated him from top to bottom with shiny ornaments and bright ribbons.

The little tree stood as tall and proud as he could. He stretched and strained and tried to stand straight and tall. But with his colored lights glowing and his shiny ornaments glittering, no one seemed to notice that he was little and crooked. People stopped their cars to admire him. The children of the house checked his lights and ornaments daily to make sure that none had blown off.

On Christmas Eve, the people of the house came out, bundled against the cold. People arrived from all around the neighborhood. Even strangers stopped to join. Softly, sweetly, they sang in harmony.

O holy night, the stars are brightly shining,
This is the night of our dear savior's birth.

As the last notes died away in the still night, there was a cooing and a whirring of wings. The people looked up and saw, perched on the very tip of the little tree, a beautiful white dove.

The dove remained on top of the tree until the last neighbor had left and the last child had gone to sleep. Then she slipped closer in among the branches and said softly, "Little Christmas tree, you gave me shelter when I was too tired to fly any further. You gave me your softest branches as a nest for my children. In doing this you caused yourself to grow crooked, and you suffered through a long, cold, lonely winter.

"When we parted, you asked me about Christmas trees, and about the meaning of Christmas. Even then, after seeing the fate of all your friends, you wanted to fulfill your destiny.

"Look down, little tree. Look at your branches. See the shiny ornaments, see the bright lights, see the footprints in the snow of all the people who came to admire you. This is your reward. For many years to come, you will stand proudly in this garden, and every Christmas you will be decorated like this and surrounded by love."

The little tree looked down. He saw himself shining in the dark. He saw the footprints in the snow of all the people who had come to share their joy around him. And he felt bigger and taller than any tree that garden had ever seen.

II

Stories of Santa Claus

THE NIGHT BEFORE CHRISTMAS

by Clement Clarke Moore
Illustrated by John Steven Gurney

Twas the night before Christmas, when all through the house
   Not a creature was stirring, not even a mouse;
The stockings were hung by the chimney with care,
   In the hopes that St. Nicholas soon would be there;

The children were nestled all snug in their beds,
  While visions of sugarplums danced in their heads;
And Mama in her 'kerchief, and I in my cap,
  Had just settled our brains for a long winter's nap;
When out on the lawn there arose such a clatter,
  I sprang from my bed to see what was the matter.

Away to the window I flew like a flash,
  Tore open the shutters and threw up the sash.
The moon on the breast of the new-fallen snow,
  Gave the lustre of midday to objects below,
When, what to my wondering eyes should appear,
  But a miniature sleigh, and eight tiny reindeer,
With a little old driver, so lively and quick,
  I knew in a moment it must be St. Nick.

More rapid than eagles his coursers they came,
    And he whistled, and shouted, and called them by name;
"Now *Dasher*! Now *Dancer*! Now, *Prancer* and *Vixen*!
    On, *Comet*! On, *Cupid*! On, *Donder* and *Blitzen*!
To the top of the porch! To the top of the wall!
    Now dash away! Dash away! Dash away all!"
As dry leaves that before the wild hurricane fly,
    When they meet with an obstacle, mount to the sky;
So up to the housetop the coursers they flew,
    With the sleigh full of toys, and St. Nicholas too.
And then in a twinkling, I heard on the roof,
    The prancing and pawing of each little hoof—

As I drew in my head and was turning around,
    Down the chimney St. Nicholas came with a bound.
He was dressed all in fur, from his head to his foot,
    And his clothes were all tarnished with ashes and soot;
A bundle of toys he had flung on his back,
    And he looked like a pedlar just opening his pack.

His eyes – how they twinkled! His dimples, how merry!
　　His cheeks were like roses, his nose like a cherry!
His droll little mouth was drawn up like a bow,
　　And the beard of his chin was as white as the snow;
The stump of a pipe he held tight in his teeth,
　　And the smoke it encircled his head like a wreath;
He had a broad face and a little round belly,
　　That shook when he laughed, like a bowlful of jelly.
He was chubby and plump, a right jolly old elf,
　　And I laughed when I saw him, in spite of myself,

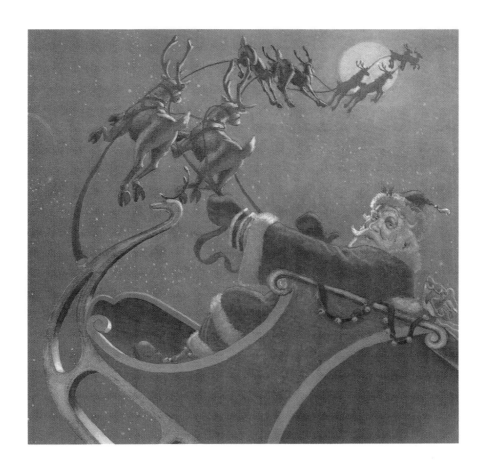

A wink of his eye and a twist of his head,
   Soon gave me to know I had nothing to dread;
He spoke not a word, but went straight to his work,
   And filled all the stockings; then turned with a jerk,
And laying his finger aside of his nose,
   And giving a nod, up the chimney he rose;
He sprang to his sleigh, to his team gave a whistle,
   And away they all flew like the down of a thistle.
But I heard him exclaim, ere he drove out of sight,
   "Happy Christmas to all. And to all a good night."

THAT'S NOT SANTA!

by Leonard Kessler

December 24 . . .

It is the day before Christmas.
Santa's sleigh is filled with toys.
Everything is ready for Santa's trip.
But where is Santa?

Santa is sleeping.

"Time to get up. Time to put on my red suit," he says.

Santa looks for his red suit. He looks everywhere.

"Have you seen my red suit?" No one has seen Santa's red suit.

"No red suit. No Christmas!"

"NO CHRISTMAS!"

"Wait. I have an idea."

"How's this?"

"Oh, no. You can't go out like that. That's not Santa!"

"Wait. Wait. I'll be right back," Santa says.

"How about this?"

"Or this?"

"This okay?
What do you think?"

"No, no, no. That's not Santa!"

"Wait. I'll be right back."

"This is it! Off I go."

"No, no, no. You can't go out in your underwear. That's not Santa!"

Mrs. Claus comes home. "You can't go out that way.
You will catch a cold."

"But he can't find his red suit."

"Red suit? Santa, I want you to open your
Christmas present right now."

"A new red suit! I'll put it right on. Thank you!"

"NOW THAT'S SANTA!"

"It's getting late. We have to go."

"We?"

"Ho-ho-ho. I'm going with you. I have a red suit, too."

"Ho-ho-ho. This Christmas will be twice as much fun!"

Is There a Santa Claus?
(Yes, Virginia, There Is a Santa Claus)

by Frances Church
Illustrated by Lucinda McQueen

On September 21, 1907, The New York Sun newspaper published a letter from Virginia O'Hanlon. The young girl wanted to know if there really was a Santa Claus. Her letter, and the answer from Frances Church, an editor at The Sun, became famous all over the world.

"We take pleasure in answering at once and thus prominently this communication below, expressing at the same time our great gratification that its faithful author is numbered among the friends of *The Sun:*

> Dear Editor:
>   I am 8 years old.
>   Some of my little friends say there is no
> Santa Claus.
>   Papa says, "If you see it in *The Sun* it's so."
>   Please tell me the truth, is there a Santa
> Claus?
>   Virginia O'Hanlon
>   115 West 95th Street

Virginia, your little friends are wrong. They have been affected by the skepticism of a skeptical age. They think that nothing can be which is not comprehensible by their little minds. All minds, Virginia, whether they be men's or children's, are little. In this great universe of ours man is a mere insect, an ant, in his intellect, as compared with the boundless world about him, as measured by the intelligence capable of grasping the whole of truth and knowledge.

Yes, Virginia, there is a Santa Claus. He exists as certainly as love and generosity and devotion exist, and you know that they abound and give to your life its highest beauty and joy. Alas! How dreary would be the world if there were no Santa Claus! It would be as dreary as if there were no Virginias. There would be no childlike faith then, no poetry, no romance to make tolerable this existence. We should have no enjoyment, except in sense and sight. The eternal light with which childhood fills the world would be extinguished.

Not believe in Santa Claus! You might as well not believe in fairies! You might get your papa to hire men to watch in all the chimneys on Christmas eve to catch Santa Claus, but even if they did not see Santa Claus coming down, what would that prove? Nobody sees Santa Claus, but that is no sign that there is no Santa Claus. The most real things in the world are those that neither children nor men can see. Did you ever see fairies dancing on the lawn? Of course not, but that's no proof that they are not there. Nobody can conceive or imagine all the wonders there are unseen and unseeable in the world.

You tear apart the baby's rattle and see what makes the noise inside, but there is a veil covering the unseen world which not the strongest man, nor even the united strength of all the strongest men that ever lived, could tear apart. Only faith, fancy, poetry, love, romance, can push aside that curtain and view and picture the supernal beauty and glory beyond. Is it all real? Ah, Virginia, in all this world there is nothing else real and abiding.

No Santa Claus! Thank God he lives, and he lives forever. A thousand years from now, Virginia, nay, ten times ten thousand years from now, he will continue to make glad the heart of childhood.

SANTA'S YUMMY CHRISTMAS

by Jolie Epstein
Illustrated by Margaret A. Hartelius

It was Christmas Eve.
Santa climbed into his sleigh.
There were lots of toys for everyone!
It was a tight fit.

Santa's first stop was in Japan.
He left a robot for Keyoshi.
Keyoshi left something for Santa, too.
It was a snack of sushi.
Santa gobbled up the sushi.
"Yummy!" said Santa.

Santa's next stop was India.
Hasib had been good all year.
Santa left him a new bicycle.
Hasib left Santa some curried chicken.
Santa gobbled up the chicken.
"Yummy!" said Santa.

Santa's sleigh raced to China.
Santa left Li a beautiful new doll.
Li left Santa two crispy eggrolls.
Santa gobbled up the eggrolls.
"Yummy!" said Santa.

Santa sped to Russia.
He left pretty pink ballet slippers for Natalia.
Then he gobbled up some blinis and cream.
"Yummy!" said Santa.

Santa's next stop was England.
He left a tea set for Maggie.
He left drums for Nigel.
Maggie and Nigel left some
plum pudding.
"Yummy!" said Santa.

Santa flew over the ocean.
He was starting to get a tummy ache.
He loosened his belt and unbuttoned
some buttons.

All over the world,
kids left him such tasty treats!
Santa could not stop eating!
He ate bagels in New York.
He ate fish chowder in Canada.
He ate apples and cheese in Australia.

Santa made his last stop in California.
Benjy and Belinda Winkler were
in their beds.
Then they heard a noise.
It was not HO-HO-HO.
It was OH-OH-OH!

The twins raced downstairs.
Santa was stuck in their chimney!
"Let's pull him out!" said Belinda.
Belinda climbed on Benjy's shoulders.
She pulled and pulled on Santa's legs.
But he did not move.

Benjy had an idea.
He blew up some balloons.
Benjy and Belinda ran up to the roof.
"Grab these!" shouted Benjy.
But Santa could not move.

The chimney dust gave Santa
an itchy, twitchy nose.
"Ah . . . ah . . . ahchooooo!"
Santa sneezed.
And out he popped!

Choo-o-o!

Up, up, up he went.
The reindeer raced to get him.

Benjy and Belinda found their
presents. Then Belinda remembered
something. "Look, Santa forgot to
eat his milk and cookies!"

SANTA'S CHRISTMAS SURPRISE

by Carol Thompson, Illustrated by Lucinda McQueen

It was Christmas Eve at the North Pole. The elves hurried to finish the toys. They put trucks and trains, bikes and balls, and all kinds of dolls into Santa's big pack.

Santa checked his list for the last time. "Good work," he said to the elves. "It's almost time for me to go!"

Santa put on his bright red suit and his warm boots. The elves polished the sleigh and hitched up the reindeer.

"One, two, three — four, five, six," counted Santa. "Where are Dasher and Dancer?"

"They're still in the stable," said the biggest elf, with a twinkle in his eye.

Santa opened the door of the stable. Then he
stopped and stared.

"Ho-ho-ho!" Santa laughed. "Here's a real
Christmas surprise — a new baby reindeer!"

The elves gathered around the baby.
"What's her name, Santa?" asked the smallest elf.
"She was born on Christmas Eve," said Santa.
"Let's call her Eve!"

Soon all eight reindeer were hitched up,
and Santa's sleigh was flying across the starry sky.
The elves waved good-bye.

"We'll be back in time for Christmas," called Santa.
He looked down at the stable and smiled.
Little Eve was the best Christmas surprise ever!

III

Happy Ho-ho-ho Holidays!

CLIFFORD'S CHRISTMAS
by Norman Bridwell

Hi! I'm Emily Elizabeth.
This is my dog Clifford.
Guess what holiday it is!

We start celebrating Christmas on Thanksgiving. Last year we went to the Thanksgiving Day parade. Clifford loved the big balloons.

At the end of the parade, Santa Claus came to town.
The Christmas season had begun!

Soon it started to snow.

My friends and I made a snowman. Clifford made one, too.

Clifford's snowman looked different.

Later we went to the pond to play ice hockey. We were having a great time until . . .

We decided that Clifford shouldn't play ice hockey any more.

Christmas was getting closer and closer. We counted the days.

One day Clifford saw some men digging up a tree.
He thought it would be a nice Christmas tree for us.

The tree was too big for our house . . . but it was just right for Clifford's.

When Clifford was taking a nap, my friends and I sneaked up on him with some mistletoe.

Surprise!

At last it was Christmas Eve.

Clifford and I hung up his stocking.
I put some presents under Clifford's tree.

That night when we were sleeping Santa came. He landed on Clifford's roof.

He walked around looking for a chimney . . .

Oops!

Clifford woke up.
He heard someone calling for help.

Clifford helped.
What a surprise!

Oh, no — the bag of toys!
It had fallen into Clifford's
water bowl.
The toys were ruined.

Clifford felt terrible. He had to do something. So he offered Santa his own Christmas presents to give to the children.

Santa smiled and patted Clifford. He told him not to worry. Then with a wave of his magic mittens, Santa made the toys new again.

After leaving some toys at my house, Santa got back in his sleigh. He said good-bye to Clifford, and away he flew until next year.

On Christmas morning Clifford
and I opened our presents. It was
a wonderful day.

And Clifford is a wonderful dog.
He makes every day Christmas Day.

MERRY CHRISTMAS, WHAT'S YOUR NAME

by Grace Maccarone and Bernice Chardiet
Illustrated by G. Brian Karas

The crossing-guard blew her whistle. Boys and girls waited behind her. It was a cold day. Tomorrow would be the first day of winter. Christmas was only four days away.

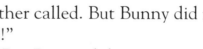

Bunny Rabissi hopped up and down to keep warm. Someone pulled her scarf, then whispered in her ear. "Go home and eat some carrots, Bunny Rabbit."

That Raymond Tally! He was always teasing Bunny about her name. She hated it. Bunny had to do something. But what?

The next morning, Bunny had an idea.

"Bunny, it's time to get up," her mother called. But Bunny did not get up.

"Bunny, are you awake? Answer me!"

But Bunny did not answer.

Mrs. Rabissi went to Bunny's room. "What's the matter?" she asked. "Why didn't you answer?"

"I'm not Bunny anymore. I've changed my name to Daisy."

"Really?" her mother said. "Well, Daisy, you'd better get up and get ready or you'll be late for school, and I'll be late for work."

At school, Daisy-Bunny found a picture of a rabbit on her desk. She knew who it was from. But she didn't care anymore. She crumpled up the picture and stuffed it in the back of her desk.

At lunchtime, Brenda asked Bunny, "Why did Ms. Darcy call you Daisy?"

"I've changed my name. My mother wrote Ms. Darcy a note about it."

"Lucky duck," said John.

Just then, Raymond came along. Daisy-Bunny put her nose in the air. "Hello, John," Raymond said.

John ignored him.

"A john is a toilet," Raymond said.

"But my name isn't John anymore. It's Jim!"

"Keep quiet, Raymond," Brenda said.

Raymond laughed as he walked away. "Look who's talking, Brenda Bolenda!"

"Did you hear what he called me?" Brenda asked. She didn't like it one bit.

That afternoon, Ms. Darcy asked, "Who will go to the calendar and mark off the shortest day of the year?" Half of the class raised their hands. Ms. Darcy called on Cynthia. Much to her surprise, two girls ran to the front of the room. Cynthia glared at Brenda, who got there first.

"The first day of winter is the shortest day of the year," Brenda said.

Ms. Darcy looked confused. "Yes, that's right, Brenda," she said, "but I called on Cynthia."

"My name is Cynthia now," Cynthia-Brenda said. "I just changed it!"

The real Cynthia gave Cynthia-Brenda a mean look. And both girls sat down.

"Copycat! Copycat!" the real Cynthia called to Cynthia-Brenda after school.

"Stop that," Cynthia-Brenda said.

But the real Cynthia would not stop. "Copycat! Copycat!"

Cynthia-Brenda chased the real Cynthia until she caught a braid.

"You pulled my hair," the real Cynthia cried. "I'm telling!"

Cynthia-Brenda knew she was in trouble as soon as she got home. Her mother had an angry look on her face. "I just spoke to Cynthia's mother," she said. "I want you to call Cynthia to apologize right now."

"No way!" Cynthia-Brenda said.

"Then go to your room," her mother said. "And don't come down until you're ready to say you're sorry."

Cynthia-Brenda had to go straight to her room.

At dinnertime, she was still there. "I'll never apologize," Cynthia-Brenda yelled, "not even if I starve to death."

Just then Cynthia-Brenda's little

brother, Truman, opened her door. "We're having fried chicken," he said.

"Go away," Cynthia-Brenda said.

A few minutes later Truman was back. "And mashed potatoes. Yum-yum."

Cynthia-Brenda tossed a pillow at Truman, but she missed.

"And chocolate layer cake for dessert!" he yelled.

That was the last straw! "I can't take it anymore!" Cynthia-Brenda said. "I'll apologize!"

Cynthia-Brenda picked up the telephone and called Cynthia.

"Oh, hello, Brenda," the real Cynthia said in a whiny voice. "And what do you have to say for yourself?"

Brenda talked as fast as she could. "You can have your stupid name back. I don't want it anyway. I'm sorry I pulled your braid. Good-bye!"

Brenda was still angry as she ate her dinner. "I hate the name Brenda!"

"It's a good name," her father said. "You should like it because it's yours."

"What are you going to call yourself now?" Truman asked.

"I don't know yet," said Brenda.

"What about Morris?" Truman said.

"That's dumb. Morris is a boy's name and I don't like it. And I don't like your name either," Brenda said.

"Who cares?" said Truman. "I changed my name to Ed."

The phone rang. Brenda went to get it.

"Hello, it's Daisy. Is Cynthia there?"

"You must have the wrong number," Brenda said, and she hung up.

The phone rang again.

"It's me, Daisy, who used to be Bunny, and I'm calling Cynthia, who used to be Brenda."

"I'm not Cynthia anymore," Brenda said. Then she had a great idea. "I'm Barbara. But you can call me Barbie."

"Oh, all right," Daisy-Bunny said, wishing that she had thought of the name Barbie first.

The next day, the boys and girls gave holiday cards to each other. Jim, who used to be John, was chosen to give them out. It was very confusing because no one could remember who was named what anymore. Even Cynthia had changed her name. Now she was Crystal.

The only one who didn't change his name was Raymond.

"Raymond Allen Tally, this card is for you," Jim-John said. Then Jim-John noticed something. "Raymond Allen Tally's initials are R.A.T.! Raymond is a rat!"

Everyone whispered, "Raymond is a rat! Raymond is a rat!" until Ms. Darcy told the class to settle down.

Barbie-Brenda raced home from school. She was glad she wasn't in trouble again. She wanted to look for her presents under the tree. She wanted to feel the smooth paper and shake the boxes and guess what was inside. Then she thought of something. The presents were all for Brenda. There wouldn't be any presents for Barbie. Changing names was a big mistake!

Brenda had to tell the others right away.

So that night Barbie went back to being Brenda. Ed went back to being Truman. Daisy went back to being Bunny. Jim went back to being John. And Crystal went back to being Cynthia.

But Raymond Allen Tally was still R.A.T.!

I SPY CHRISTMAS
by Jean Marzollo
Illustrated by Walter Wick

*Can you find everything
in the rhyme?*

I spy a clock, a bumpy
green pickle,
Santa on a sleigh and
a face on a nickel;
A frog on a leaf, a chubby
teddy bear,
Black and white keys, and
a yellow-red pear.

I spy a glove, a horse,
and a gate,
A silver coin, the shadow
of a skate;
A shovel, a lamb,
a Christmas tree light,
Five jacks, and a dove
in the dark silent night.

Dinosaurs' Christmas
by Liza Donnelly

"Bones! Let's go sledding!"

"Did you know that dinosaurs lived before the Ice Ages?"
"The last Ice Age began about one hundred thousand years ago. And the early dinosaurs lived about two hundred million years ago!"

"This is a good hill."

"Whoaaaa!"

"Aheeee!"

"Aaaaahh!"

"Eeeee!"

"Ooooh!"

"Yikes!"

"It's . . . a Plateosaurus!"

"Hi!"
"Where are we?"
"The North Pole."
"There's trouble in Santa's workshop and they need your help."
"Santa's helpers are making toy dinosaurs."

"And look, Bones, they're making them all wrong!"

"Wait!"
"Let me help!"
"This Othnielia did not have a beak, but a round nose."
"While the Pteranodon *did* have a large beak!"

"This Nodosaurus didn't have wings."

"Bactrosaurus had only one tail!"

"And the Kentrosaurus had many spikes, but not on its face."

"It's late — I wonder where Santa is?"

"The reindeer all have the flu!"
"How are we going to get the toys to all the kids?

It's impossible if Santa can't fly!"

"My friend Plateosaurus will help."

"Now Plateosaurus! Now Pteranodon!
Now Nodosaurus! And Pentaceratops!
On Bactrosaurus! On Stegoceras!
On Kentrosaurus and Othnielia!"

"Merry Christmas!"

"Wow! This was the best Christmas ever!"

IV

Christmas Songs and Carols

HARK! THE HERALD ANGELS SING

Illustrated by Lucinda McQueen

Hark! the herald angels sing,
"Glory to the new born King!
Peace on earth, and mercy mild,
God and sinners reconciled."
Joyful, all ye nations, rise,
Join the triumph of the skies;
With th'angelic host proclaim,
"Christ is born in Bethlehem."
Hark! the herald angels sing,
"Glory to the new born King!"

Christ by highest heav'n adored;
Christ the everlasting Lord;
Late in time behold Him come,
Offspring of the favored one.
Veiled in flesh, the Godhead see;
Hail th'incarnate Deity,
Please as man with men to dwell,
Jesus our Immanuel!
Hark! the herald angels sing,
"Glory to the new born King!"

Hail! the heav'n-born Prince of Peace!
Hail! the Son of Righteousness!
Light and life to all He brings,
Ris'n with healing in His wings.
Mild He lays His glory by,
Born that man no more may die,
Born to raise the sons of earth,
Born to give them second birth.
Hark! the herald angels sing,
"Glory to the new born King!"

DECK THE HALLS

Illustrated by Christine Powers

Deck the halls with boughs of holly,
Fa, la, la, la, la,
La, la, la, la.

'Tis the season to be jolly,
Fa, la, la, la, la,
La, la, la, la.

Don we now our gay apparel,
Fa, la, la, la, la, la,
La, la, la.

Troll the ancient Yuletide carol,
Fa, la, la, la, la,
La, la, la, la.

THE TWELVE DAYS OF CHRISTMAS

Illustrated by Christine Powers

On the first day of Christmas, my true love gave to me, a partridge in a pear tree.

On the second day of Christmas, my true love gave to me, two turtle doves, and a partridge in a pear tree.

On the third day of Christmas, my true love gave to me, three French hens, two turtle doves, and a partridge in a pear tree.

On the fourth day of Christmas, my true love gave to me, four calling birds, three French hens, two turtle doves, and a partridge in a pear tree.

On the fifth day of Christmas, my true love gave to me, five golden rings! four calling birds, three French hens, two turtle doves, and a partridge in a pear tree.

On the sixth day of Christmas, my true love gave to me, six geese a-laying, five golden rings! four calling birds, three French hens, two turtle doves, and a partridge in a pear tree.

On the seventh day of Christmas, my true love gave to me, seven swans a-swimming, six geese a-laying, five golden rings! four calling birds, three French hens, two turtle doves, and a partridge in a pear tree.

On the eighth day of Christmas, my true love gave to me, eight maids

a-milking, seven swans a-swimming, six geese a-laying, five golden rings! four calling birds, three French hens, two turtle doves, and a partridge in a pear tree.

On the ninth day of Christmas, my true love gave to me, nine ladies dancing, eight maids a-milking, seven swans a-swimming, six geese a-laying, five golden rings! four calling birds, three French hens, two turtle doves, and a partridge in a pear tree.

On the tenth day of Christmas, my true love gave to me, ten lords a-leaping, nine ladies dancing, eight maids a-milking, seven swans a-swimming, six geese a-laying, five golden rings! four calling birds, three French hens, two turtle doves, and a partridge in a pear tree.

On the eleventh day of Christmas, my true love gave to me, eleven pipers piping, ten lords a-leaping, nine ladies dancing, eight maids a-milking, seven swans a-swimming, six geese a-laying, five golden rings! four calling birds, three French hens, two turtle doves, and a partridge in a pear tree.

On the twelfth day of Christmas, my true love gave to me, twelve drummers drumming, eleven pipers piping, ten lords a-leaping, nine ladies dancing, eight maids a-milking, seven swans a-swimming, six geese a-laying, five golden rings! four calling birds, three French hens, two turtle doves, and a partridge in a pear tree.

SILENT NIGHT

Illustrated by Lucinda McQueen

Silent night, Holy night,
All is calm, all is bright;
'Round yon virgin mother and child,
Holy infant so tender and mild,
Sleep in heavenly peace,
Sleep in heavenly peace.

Silent night, Holy night,
Shepherds quake at the sight;
Glories stream from heaven afar,
Heav'nly hosts sing Alleluia!
Christ the savior is born,
Christ the savior is born.

Silent night, Holy night,
Son of God, love's pure light;
Radiance beams from Thy holy face,
With the dawn of redeeming grace,
Jesus, Lord at Thy birth,
Jesus, Lord at Thy birth.

Jingle Bells

Illustrated by Christine Powers

Dashing through the snow
In a one-horse open sleigh,
O'er the fields we go,
Laughing all the way.

Bells on bob-tail ring,
Making spirits bright;
What fun it is to ride and sing
A sleighing song tonight!

Jingle bells, jingle bells,
Jingle all the way!
Oh, what fun it is to ride
In a one-horse open sleigh!

Jingle bells, jingle bells,
Jingle all the way!
Oh, what fun it is to ride
In a one-horse open sleigh!

JOY TO THE WORLD!

Illustrated by Joe Boddy

Joy to the world! the Lord is come.
Let the earth receive the King.
Let ev'ry heart prepare Him room,
And heav'n and nature sing,
And heav'n and nature sing,
And heaven and heaven and nature sing.

Joy to the world! the Savior reigns.
Let men their songs employ.
While fields and floods, rocks, hills, and plains,
Repeat the sounding joy,
Repeat the sounding joy,
Repeat, repeat the sounding joy.

He rules the world with truth and grace,
And makes the nations prove
The glories of His righteousness,
And wonders of His love,
And wonders of His love,
And wonders, and wonders of His love.

WE WISH YOU A MERRY CHRISTMAS

Illustrated by Christine Powers

We wish you a Merry Christmas,
We wish you a Merry Christmas,
We wish you a Merry Christmas,
And a Happy New Year.
Glad tidings we bring
To you and your kin;
Glad tidings for Christmas
And a Happy New Year.

Oh, bring us some figgy pudding,
Oh, bring us some figgy pudding,
Oh, bring us some figgy pudding,
And bring it right here.

We won't go until we get some,
We won't go until we get some,
We won't go until we get some,
So bring some right here.

We all like our figgy pudding,
We all like our figgy pudding,
We all like our figgy pudding,
With all its good cheer.

We wish you a Merry Christmas,
We wish you a Merry Christmas,
We wish you a Merry Christmas,
And a Happy New Year.
Glad tidings we bring
To you and your kin;
Glad tidings for Christmas
And a Happy New Year.

O LITTLE TOWN OF BETHLEHEM

Illustrated by Joe Boddy

O little town of Bethlehem,
How still we see thee lie;
Above thy deep and dreamless sleep
The silent stars go by.
Yet in thy dark streets shineth
The everlasting light;
The hopes and fears of all the years
Are met in thee tonight.

For Christ is born of Mary,
And gathered all above,
While mortals sleep, the angels keep
Their watch of wond'ring love.
O morning stars, together
Proclaim the holy birth,
And praises sing to God, the King,
And peace to men on earth.

How silently, how silently
The wondrous gift is given!
So God imparts to human hearts
The blessing of His heav'n.
No ear may hear His coming;
But in this world of sin,
Where meek souls will receive Him, still
The dear Christ enters in.

O Holy Child of Bethlehem,
Descend to us, we pray;
Cast out our sin, and enter in,
Be born in us today.
We hear the Christmas angels
The great glad tidings tell.
O come to us, abide with us,
Our Lord Immanuel.

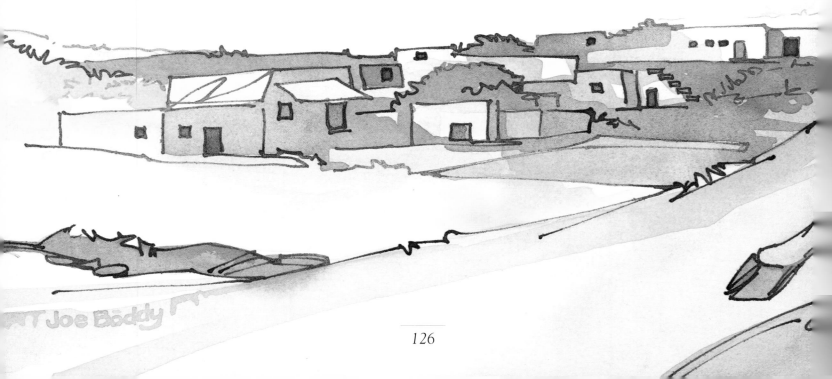